# My Gr Words

## Consultants

**Ashley Bishop, Ed.D.**

**Sue Bishop, M.E.D.**

## Publishing Credits

Dona Herweck Rice, *Editor-in-Chief*

Robin Erickson, *Production Director*

Lee Aucoin, *Creative Director*

Sharon Coan, *Project Manager*

Jamey Acosta, *Editor*

Rachelle Cracchiolo, M.A.Ed., *Publisher*

W9-DJD-415

**Image Credits**

cover Kyrylo Grekov/Shutterstock; p.2 irin-k/Shutterstock; p.3 berna namoglu/Shutterstock; p.5 Maksym Bondarchuk/Shutterstock; p.6 karam Miri/Shutterstock; p.7 Demid Borodin/Shutterstock; p.8 Sandra Van Der Steen/Dreamstime; p.9 Tomas Sereda/Dreamstime; p.10 Kyrylo Grekov/Shutterstock; back cover Sandra Van Der Steen/Dreamstime

## Teacher Created Materials

5301 Oceanus Drive
Huntington Beach, CA 92649-1030
http://www.tcmpub.com

**ISBN 978-1-4333-3980-6**

**Look at the grass.**

# Where is the grass?

# Look at green.

# Where is green?

# Look at the grill.

# Where is the grill?

**Look at the grasshopper.**

# Where is the grasshopper?

**Look at the grapes.**

# Glossary

grapes

grass

grasshopper

green

grill

# Sight Words

Look    at    the    Where    is

# Activities

- Read the book aloud to your child, pointing to the *gr* words. Help your child describe where the *gr* objects are found.

- Play Red Light, Green Light with your child. To play this game, say "green light" for your child to go. Say "red light" for your child to stop.

- Set up an obstacle course on the grass for your child. Have your child run around boxes, cones, buckets, or hoops.

- Buy some grapes, wash them in a bowl, and watch them float. Have your child eat them for a snack.

- Help your child think of a personally valuable word to represent the letters *gr*, such as *grin*.